MW01531967

The House by the Creek

by

Rich Leonard

For the Tilly boys.

Dean Leonard

Tudor Publishers
Greensboro

The House by the Creek by Rich Leonard © 2012

First Edition

Library of Congress Cataloging-in-Publication Data

Leonard, Rich, 1964-
   The house by the creek / by Rich Leonard. — 1st ed.
      p. cm.
   Summary: While Valentine Leonhardt and his three eldest sons fight against the British in 1781, his wife, three daughters, and two young sons remain behind to run their Guilford County, North Carolina, farm.
   ISBN 978-0-9778026-5-4 (alk. paper)
   [1. Soldiers—Fiction. 2. Farm life—North Carolina—Fiction. 3. Family
life—North Carolina—Fiction. 4. Guilford Courthouse, Battle of, N.C.,
1781—Fiction. 5. North Carolina—History—Revolution, 1775-1783—Fiction.]   I.
Title.
   PZ7.L5512Hou 2012
   [Fic]—dc23

                                                        2012030587

To my five children,
Matthew, Justin, Louise Gray, Elizabeth and Cain,
who carry forward the genes of their forebears.

Contents

Chapter 1

The Secret

A firm hand on his shoulder woke Jacob from a deep sleep. In the early morning light, he was surprised to see the strong face of his father standing over him. Valentine Leonhardt rarely climbed the ladder to the sleeping loft Jacob shared with his brothers.

His father put a finger to Jacob's lips. "Be quiet, my son. Wake no one and come with me."

Rubbing his eyes, Jacob followed his father down the steep ladder to the main room of the Leonhardt log house. They went down another set of broad stairs to the basement kitchen. It was so early that not even Mother was awake.

"Jacob, there is a secret I must show you, and it must be the most important secret of your life," said Father.

"Yes, Father." Jacob was curious about why Father had awakened him and brought him alone to the kitchen, but like all of his brothers and sisters, had learned to wait. Father always explained.

"Jacob, go to the corner of the kitchen to the left of the fireplace, and count down nine logs."

Now Jacob was completely baffled, but did as he was told. He moved to the corner of the massive hearth, and carefully counted.

"Does that log appear different?" asked Valentine.

Jacob studied the log carefully. There must be some trick here, but no matter how hard he looked, he could not see it. "No, Father."

"Now watch what I do," said Valentine He reached into the fireplace and grabbed the tongs. Several inches from the wall, he placed the tongs on the ninth log and gently pulled. A piece of the log about a foot long slid out.

"Look, Jacob. What do you see?" Valentine handed him the piece of log.

Jacob studied it carefully, turning it completely around. "It looks just like a regular piece of wood, Father, but it is uncommonly heavy."

His father smiled. "That is a very smart thing to notice, Jacob, and that is the secret. Look closely at this end. See where there is a plug in the wood? This log is hollow, son, and in it is all of the gold our family possesses. It is the future of our family. And only you and I know it."

Jacob was stunned. "But Father, we must go now and tell Mother. She is in charge when you are away, and she will need to know this."

Valentine grabbed Jacob's shoulders, his face stern. "Hear me, boy. This is the most important thing I have ever said to you. Evil men may come here while I and your brothers are away, and threaten to do unkind things to your mother and sisters to force them to tell where our treasure is hidden. Mother must not know, and your sisters must not know. They are safer not knowing."

Jacob's eyes grew wide with fear. His father continued. "But if they come, they will not suspect that a small boy knows such a secret. I know that you are brave and smart, Jacob, and you can do this for our family."

"Why do I need to know, Father? Mother says you are only going to fight for a short time and will be home."

Valentine dropped to one knee and put his arms around Jacob. "Son, Mother is right; I plan to be home soon. But you must understand that this is a war, and sometimes men do not return from war."

Jacob's eyes widened as he finally understood what Father was saying. Unable to stop himself, he threw his arms around his father's neck and broke into loud sobs. A world without Father was unimaginable.

"I know, son," Valentine said. "It is too much for a small boy. But these are hard times, and you must be brave."

"But Father, what if . . . ? What if . . . ?" He could not say aloud the possibility that his father would not return.

"Jacob, if I do not return, say nothing to anyone until the fighting is over. Then, bring your oldest brother who comes home down here and show him what I have shown you. And when you do this, you will have saved your family's future."

His father gave Jacob a final hug and rose from his knee. "Now, back up the ladder with you. Sleep a few more minutes before it is time for breakfast. I must speak to your mother before we depart."

Chapter 2

Morning of Departure

Valentine quietly placed the piece of log back into its secret place, checked again to make sure no one could see the seam, and looked around the spacious basement kitchen and dining area. Twenty-five years earlier, he and Elizabeth had traveled to this spot in the North Carolina wilderness with only a promise of land and their dreams. They had slept the first night in the open air beside the creek, on this very ground where their fine three-story house now stood. They had prospered beyond all imagining, with acres of fallow land, cattle, horses, good neighbors and a church, and best of all, eight fine children. It was not bad for a poor German immigrant who had almost gone bankrupt as a Philadelphia tailor before coming to North Carolina. Now he must fight to keep it.

He slowly went up the wide plank stairs to the main floor and entered the bedroom he shared with his wife. "Did you sleep well, Wife?" he asked.

She responded with a tired smile. "I did not close my eyes all night, as you well know, Husband."

They had talked late into the night as she had gently asked him to reconsider his decision to go with their sons to join General Greene's army to fight the British.

"Valentine, you are not a young man. And I am sending my three oldest sons into this army. No one can doubt our commitment to this cause." She spoke over the quiet clicking of her knitting needles. Not once in twenty-five years had he seen her hands idle.

"Elizabeth, you know I am the best shot in Rowan County, and can wrestle any of our sons to the ground." He rarely bragged, but was proud that at the age of fifty-eight had retained all of his physical prowess.

She smiled. "I do not doubt your stamina, Husband. But there are other issues here." Unsaid was that he would be leaving her with a farm to manage and a household of three daughters and two small sons to look after. She was not a timid woman, and did not doubt her ability to handle anything that came her way. Still, there was a war going on.

"My age saves me here, dear. The militia has allowed me only a sixty-day enlistment, and I promise to be home at the end. But the battle with Cornwallis will be in that sixty days, and I must be a part of it. The boys must stay for six months, but they will be home for the harvest." He began removing his boots and preparing for bed.

She put away her knitting and began to unlace her cap. "Then go with God's grace and mine, Valentine. We will be here when you return." And they had gone to bed, but with little sleep.

Now this morning, as she laced her cap to start the day, the discussion was over. "We must get moving, Husband. I looked yesterday, and if we are to plant a crop this spring, ploughing must begin in the lower fields as soon as the four of you take your leave. We can't all be going for a horseback ride through the country today."

Chapter 3

The Sleeping Loft

Jacob could hear his big brothers beginning to stir in the sleeping loft. His little brother Philip, with whom he shared a straw mattress, slept soundly beside him.

"What will happen today, Peter?" said his third brother, father's namesake Valentine, who was called Val and at seventeen was as big as Father and equally strong and serious.

"I overheard Father talking to Mr. Fritz yesterday, so I know the plan. The four of us will leave after breakfast and go to the church to meet Mr. Fritz and Mr. Klontz and their sons. Father will say a prayer for our safety, and then we will all ride together to the square in Salisbury where we will join the Rowan militia." His oldest brother, Peter, packed his knapsack as he spoke. Already twenty, Peter often volunteered on other farms during planting and harvesting, and usually knew what was going on in the community. As he spoke, he kicked the sleeping body on the pallet beside him.

"Get up, Michael. We leave directly after breakfast, and you must be packed by then." Michael's ability to sleep was legendary in the family. Often he was absent from meals, only to be caught napping in the barn loft. Michael was Jacob's favorite brother. He always allowed Jacob to climb up on the front of his saddle to ride, and no one teased Jacob when Michael was in earshot.

"Then what do we do, big brother? Just march around Salisbury and wave to the ladies, I guess." Michael laughed loudly, still wrapped in his blanket on his pallet.

"So you wish," retorted Peter, kicking him more forcefully this time. "General Cornwallis is on the march from South Carolina, and General Greene has orders to stop him before he reaches Virginia. Our militia will join General Greene to do this. Now get moving."

"Are you frightened, Peter?" asked Val. "I have been awake most of the night trying to understand all of this."

"Just a bit, little brother. This is a war, and it is serious. But we can hunt and shoot as well as any men in the county, and this is our land. We know every tree and stream. I am more concerned about leaving Mother here alone with our sisters and brothers."

"But some of our neighbors are not fighting. Yesterday Reid said his father would not allow him to go, and thinks we should not either." Reid Clodfelter was Val's best friend. His parents had emigrated from Germany on the *Neptune*, the same ship that had brought the Leonhardts to America, and they farmed nearby. Val would do whatever Father said, but was having difficulty understanding why.

"Val, Father would never send us into harm's way unless he thought it the right thing to do. He says he came to this country to be free, and so that his sons and daughters can live free. That can never happen if we must live under the thumb of an English king." Peter put his arm around his brother's shoulder as he spoke. "We will be together, and it will be fine."

Michael suddenly threw off his blanket. "Don't be so serious, Val. I would fight for the Tsar of Russia if it would let me miss the spring ploughing. Now let's go. I'm hungry. And I packed last night, Peter, so quit kicking me."

The three brothers raced down the ladder to the kitchen where breakfast would soon be waiting.

Chapter 4

The Sisters' Room

In the bedroom they shared on the main floor of the house, the sisters were stirring. As was true most mornings, they lay quietly talking in the warmth of the big feather bed they shared.

"I cannot believe that Father and our brothers are leaving today," sighed Barbara, the eldest. "Our family has never been separated before."

"Quit pretending to be so unhappy, dear sister," retorted Catherine, at sixteen the next oldest. "I will miss Father, but will enjoy some time without the teasing of our rapscallion brothers. And besides, you are not sad that they are leaving, but only that Thomas Fritz is going with them." Thomas lived on the nearby farm, and at church on Sundays, he and Barbara could scarcely keep their eyes off each other.

Barbara's attempt to smother her sister with her pillow was interrupted by their mother entering the room. "Girls, stop this foolishness and get dressed quickly. We have much to do. Barbara, go to the smokehouse and cut a nice slab of ham to fry for breakfast. Catherine, gather all of the fresh eggs from the henhouse. And Eliza, come with me and we will start the porridge and griddle cakes."

Eliza's eyes grew wide. "Mother, it sounds like Christmas breakfast."

Elizabeth reached down and hugged her youngest child. Although she was careful never to play favorites, her affection for Eliza was always obvious, and was shared by the whole family. "This is no holiday, little one, but your father and brothers need a good meal before they start on their journey."

Barbara and Catherine raced down the front steps into the chill of a foggy February morning that would soon burn off and give way to pleasant sunshine. "At least the journey will be pleasant from here to Salisbury," said Barbara. "It would be dreadful if they were to leave in the ice and snow."

"I'd go by dog sled if only I could go with them," responded Catherine. "Why do we girls have to stay home and do the same old chores while the boys go gallavanting around the countryside fighting the Tories?" Catherine picked up a stone and hurled it at the large oak tree on the other side of the creek, cheered by the resounding "thunk." She could throw, shoot and ride as well as any boy her age.

Barbara leaned her head toward her sister, and whispered. "I think you will be surprised. I heard Mother and Father talking, and there is to be something new in our future."

Catherine quickly responded. "What is it? No keeping secrets."

"Well, it seems that with the boys gone, and the spring season upon us, you and I are going to learn how to plough."

Barbara laughed at her sister's dismayed face, and continued, "I'm sure it will be no problem for a girl with your ability."

Laughing, the girls ran through the barnyard to gather their items for the family breakfast.

Chapter 5

First Encounter

Miles south of the Leonardt farm, General Greene had just finished his first inspection of the army he had been sent by General Washington to command. He was dismayed.

"Ye gods, man," he said to his new personal aide beside him. "Is this ragtag group of misfits the Army of the South that is expected to defeat Cornwallis? There are scarcely five hundred men here, and many are sick and ill-fitted."

"I am afraid so, General. When Charleston fell, most of the South Carolina militia gave up hope of winning and returned home to protect their property and families. But it is not as gloomy as it might appear. The call has gone out for the North Carolina militia to assemble and join with you, and right now, they are gathering in Salisbury and Hillsborough to await your orders." Lieutenant Boger, General Greene's aide, had done his homework.

"But can we count on them to leave their farms and join us?" queried General Greene.

"I believe so, General. Remember King's Mountain, when the North Carolina mountain men appeared out of the woods and destroyed Colonel Tarleton's regiment."

"That was truly a great day for our cause, Boger. But this is much bigger. Cornwallis is headed this way with two thousand British troops, the best-trained soldiers in the

17

world. He plans to sweep through North Carolina into Virginia, divide our new country into half, and end the rebellion. He must be stopped, or we may both spend our last days in a British prison."

Lieutenant Boger responded forcefully. "I know the men of this region, sir. I grew up among them, on the banks of the Yadkin River which we must soon cross. They are independent and prize their freedom, and they will follow you. You will see."

General Greene laughed. "The only thing following me now is General Cornwallis' army, and we are about to engage in a game of hide-and-seek to make sure it does not find us until the militia arrives. I trust it's a game Southern lads know?"

Boger laughed in response, with growing respect for his new general. "We are masters at it. He will never find us until we are ready to be found."

Chapter 6

The Church

Eleven men gathered in the yard in front of the small church where they all worshiped. In addition to the four Leonhardts, Mr Klontz and Mr. Fritz were there, each with two of their sons. Matthew, the Fritz's indentured servant, had also come. The church was a small but dignified structure, with a peaked roof, a large wooden door, and a glass window in the front over the small table where the cross stood. The women of the community had insisted that the church be built even before the houses were finished. As Mr. Klontz often joked, "The women wanted our souls fed before our bodies."

Each Sunday, the local Lutheran families gathered to read scripture and sing hymns. Twice a year, the minister from Salisbury came to conduct a long morning service, followed by a feast on the church grounds.

Today, though, no one was festive. Although they had waited for more than an hour, no one else arrived. Messages had gone out to every farm in the area of the dire need to assemble and join the militia, but many of their neighbors had chosen to stay home.

"Gentlemen, I suggest that we go inside for a moment of prayer, then be on our way." Although the local community had no organized government, everyone deferred to

Valentine to take charge.

"Father, before we go inside, what exactly is our plan?" Val, the youngest of the group and ever serious, was trying to figure out how this new adventure would go.

"It is fairly simple, son. After we pray, we will leave by horseback and ride two days to Salisbury. There, we will meet up with General Greene and his army, and the rest of the North Carolina militia. Matthew will carefully return by back roads with all of our horses. The militia will march on foot."

Valentine turned to enter the church, but Peter had a question. "Father, why are we sending our horses home? We will be no match for the British cavalry on foot."

"What we are called on to do is fight the British infantry, son, not the cavalry. They will be on foot just as we. And there may be no food or forage for our horses, and we cannot risk that they may be injured or killed in battle. We will need them when this war is over. Now let's go inside before we lose any more daylight."

The men entered the small sanctuary, removing their hats as they crossed the threshold. They moved to the front and knelt.

Valentine began to pray. "Our Heavenly Father, look kindly on us as we go forth to battle, and know we go not out of malice or ill will. We desire only to live peacefully in this new land, in harmony with each other and in obedience to Your laws. But having fled from persecution in our homeland, we now find our lives disrupted by the unreasonable actions of the British King. He has oppressed us beyond all reason. He requires us to pay a poll tax for every man, woman and child in the colony, only so that his royal governor may live in a mansion of sinful luxury at New Bern. And when we cannot pay it, he has sent his assessors among us to seize our livestock and land for forced sale. Now his army threatens our very land. Be with us in our battle, and if it be Thy will, deliver us of a great victory as you did for your people of Israel so long ago. Amen."

"Nicely said, Valentine," said Mr. Fritz, rising from his knees. He was Valentine's oldest friend. "I am always amazed that a poor Philadelphia tailor can speak with such eloquence. You help us all see what we are about."

Valentine smiled. "What we must be about now, my friend, is getting to Salisbury. Let's get mounted." The small band rode out of the churchyard, each wondering, without saying, when he would see it again.

Chapter 7

The Creek

Jacob, Philip and Eliza were racing boats in the creek, their favorite game. Eliza was shrieking with excitement, for unlike the usual outcome where she lagged behind her older brothers, today she was winning.

The game was simple. Each child had a wooden boat carved by Valentine, and a long stick that could reach the water of the creek, even from its steepest bank. Boats were put in at the top of the rapids behind the barn, and one could only use your stick if your boat became stuck. But there was a trick. Each player could only free the boat when all three boats became stuck. And today, Philip's boat was caught far back on a rock, and Jacob's was trapped behind a fallen branch. Eliza's boat sailed on down the creek, and the frustrated boys could only watch as her boat approached the finish line, the large chestnut tree where the creek widened into a pond.

Eliza reached down and plucked her boat out of the water, and ran toward the house. "Mother, come quick. I need to tell you something right now."

Elizabeth raced down the steps, certain that someone was hurt. Cuts and bruises were common among her boisterous tribe. "What is all this yelling about, little one?"

"I won, Mother, I won, for the first time. I beat the boys!" Eliza still could not believe her good fortune.

Philip and Jacob approached the steps carrying their boats, each a bit dejected.

Eliza raced to them and said, "Let's do it again, right now. I bet I can win a second time."

Elizabeth intervened. "Play time is over, children. It's time for chores. Get the water buckets and fill up the troughs in the barn for the calves and lambs. They will be thirsty by now. And no more playing in the creek today. Just fill your buckets."

The creek was the center of life on the farm. Curving in a large horseshoe around the house, at places it settled into deep pools where catfish and bream could be caught. At other places, it ran shallow over large rocks that were perfect for wading. Even on the driest days of summer it provided plenty of clean water for the family and their livestock. Unlike their neighbors, the Leonhardts had never needed to dig a well.

Past the house, it widened into a pond behind a small dam that Valentine and the other men in the community had built years before. Water raced through the chute at the side of the dam to turn the wheel of the gristmill. Each fall, the mill was used to grind corn into meal for all of the neighbors. The pond was a favorite swimming hole for the older boys, particularly on a hot day after threshing wheat.

Each Saturday afternoon, Elizabeth gave Valentine and her older sons a choice. Either take the soap and bathe in the mill pond, or suffer the indignity of washing in her large tub in the kitchen. No Leonhardt would cross the threshold of the church on the Sabbath who was unwashed. Except on the coldest Saturdays of the year, the men always chose to dive into the pond.

Elizabeth often claimed that the creek was her best friend, and talked to her all day long. At her suggestion, Valentine had built for her a wooden box with a tight lid.

She surprised him by submerging it in a pool where a spring that fed the creek emerged from the ground. In it, she kept milk, butter and cheese that stayed cool and fresh. Each Monday, she placed her washing pot near the shallow rocks and built a fire underneath it. She then placed the hot, soapy clothes on the shallow rocks to rinse them. Elizabeth did not like to spend a night anywhere else, for she said she could scarcely sleep without the sound of the creek to calm her. For everyone, it was the sound of home.

Chapter 8

An Unhappy General

At his camp near Charlotte, General Cornwallis was unhappy. "So, Governor Martin, where are the thousands of loyalists you promised would rise to my side when I entered North Carolina? So far, this place has been nothing but a hornet's nest, with my troops harassed and attacked at every turn."

Across from him sat His Excellency, Josiah Martin, the royal governor of the colony of North Carolina. He had been summoned by an angry General Cornwallis, and had just arrived in his ornate coach from his palace in New Bern. He was dressed for the occasion, in a brocade suit and formal wig.

"I cannot explain it, my Lord. I issued a very clear proclamation that required the citizens of this colony to come to your aid. I am told it was distributed widely." Governor Martin rarely left his palace at New Bern, where he was famous for ruling by royal edict throughout the colony.

"A pox on your Proclamation. Do you have reason to believe that I may expect assistance in the coming days?" Cornwallis marched back and forth across the small parlor of the house he had seized for his headquarters as he spoke, visibly upset.

Governor Martin was equally irritated, unaccustomed to

being challenged in any way. "I cannot do more than I have already done, General. But I do think as you move north toward Hillsborough, more citizens will come to your assistance. The area around Charlotte has always been rebellious."

"We shall see, Governor," said Cornwallis, now with a sly smile on his face. "And I assume that you will remain with the army as we travel north to make certain that this happens?"

Governor Martin was horrified. He was not a military man, and the rough coach ride across the state had already exhausted him. "General, there would be little point in that. I must return to New Bern. I have a colony to govern."

Cornwallis was unrelenting. "Governor, unless I am successful, there will be no colony for you or any other Englishman to rule. Surely you would like for the King to know of your every effort in these critical days?"

Realizing that he had been outflanked, Governor Martin agreed. It was well-known that the general had the ear of the British Prime Minister, who in turn had the ear of the king. Crossing swords with General Cornwallis had ended the career of others.

"Thank you, Governor. Get a good night's sleep. We ride soon. I cannot abide many more days in this godforsaken town." Then the general bowed deeply to the governor, who in fact outranked him in the British command, and left to meet with his senior staff.

Chapter 9

Unwanted Visitors

From their perch high in an apple tree in the orchard, Philip and Jacob saw three horsemen approaching the house. They scurried down. Visitors were rare, especially with Father and their brothers away.

Elizabeth was standing inside the house, speaking to three strangers on the porch through the open top of the double door. The bottom of the door remained firmly closed.

"Good morning, madam," said one of the visitors, a slight man dressed in usual garb but wearing a strange silk cap on his head. "Might I inquire where I might find your husband?"

"Good day, gentlemen. I am afraid that my husband is away on business. What may I do for you today?"

"This business that has taken your husband from home, madam, will it keep him away long?" As he spoke, the gentleman was surveying the house and yard to see who else might be near.

As Elizabeth started to reply, Philip excitedly spoke up. "Father has gone to Salisbury to find General Greene, and then they are going hunting together."

The men laughed. "And what would your father and General Greene be hunting, boy?" asked the visitor.

Philip shrugged. "I don't know, sir. I didn't hear that part."

The man turned back to Elizabeth and spoke sternly. "Madam, I am Colonel David Fanning of the royal militia, and I have been commanded by Governor Martin to commandeer supplies for the British army that will soon be in this area. As a loyal citizen of this colony, I am sure you will do your part."

"Gentlemen, we have very little, and what we have I need to feed my family until the next harvest," said Elizabeth. "But you are guests here, and I will be glad to give you some provisions for your meal today."

Colonel Fanning sneered. "I think you are much too modest, madam. This looks to be a prosperous farm, with cattle and orchards, and even a gristmill. I am certain you have more to offer us. I suspect there may even be a bit of gold and silver about."

Mother scoffed. "We are farmers, Colonel. We trade in corn and pigs, not gold and silver."

Catherine came hurrying across the yard, returning to the house for lunch after a morning of ploughing. As she stepped up onto the porch, Colonel Fanning roughly grabbed her arm. "Madam, perhaps if your lovely daughter were to go for a short ride with us, you might soften your view about assisting us." The colonel and his two henchmen laughed crudely.

As Catherine futilely tried to pull away, Elizabeth said, "Perhaps I do have something. Wait here."

Jacob was torn. Father had told him he must never reveal where the gold and silver were hidden, but surely Father never considered that Catherine might be taken.

He started to speak as Elizabeth returned, her hands beneath her large apron. She held out a small purse and handed it to Colonel Fanning. "My husband left me these few coins to buy corn for seed if he has not returned by planting time. The rats ransacked our crib this winter and we have little left. And there are two hams in the smokehouse that you may take. That is all we have."

"That is not sufficient, madam . . ."

Before Fanning could continue, Elizabeth raised her other hand from under her apron. In it, she held Valentine's pistol, and pointed it at Colonel Fanning's head. "Let my child go, Colonel, or be prepared to meet your Maker. I shoot straight, as many a fox bothering my henhouse can attest. Children, all of you come in the house this instant."

Colonel Fanning stood frozen, still holding Catherine's arm.

"I do not jest, Colonel. Your men may kill us all, but you will not be alive to see it." Elizabeth held the pistol steady, scarcely a yard from the colonel's head.

Fanning laughed and released Catherine's arm. "It is fortunate for you, madam, that I appreciate a spirited lady. We will take what you offer, and cause you no further inconvenience, at least not this day."

As the men rode away, the children gathered about their mother in the main room. Catherine was quietly crying.

Elizabeth remained calm. "Catherine, be still, and help me get lunch on the table. And Philip, young boys should be seen and not heard when adults are speaking. It is over, at least for today."

Chapter 10

First Night in Camp

Lieutenant Boger made his way slowly among the campfires of the new troops who had just arrived to join the North Carolina militia. Although fewer had come than hoped, still it was encouraging to see enthusiastic and well-equipped new soldiers.

At one fire, the Leonhardts, Fritzes, and Klontzes were talking quietly. The trip from Salisbury had been uneventful, and Matthew had left for home with all of the horses.

Val was disturbed by the condition of his fellow soldiers. "I feel sorry for many of these men, Father. They have almost no clothing, many are almost barefooted, and I have heard that they have eaten little in weeks. Perhaps we should share our supplies with them."

"That is a Christian thought, Val, but not a wise one," replied Valentine. "Our supplies would do little to aid the entire army, and in a few days we would be in the same condition. We came to fight, and to do that, we must remain equipped and fed."

"But what are we doing here, Father?" asked Peter. "When will we know the plan?"

The older men all chuckled. "Welcome to the life of a private, Peter. Only the general knows the plan, and I'm certain at times we will be very perplexed by his decisions. But we must have faith in his leadership." Mr. Klontz leaned back on his pack, savoring his last pipe of the day. The older men would not admit it, but they were enjoying their respite from the daily labor of their farms.

"Good evening, gentlemen," said a tall stranger as he approached their fire. "Might I warm my hands a moment with you? There is a chill in the air tonight." Lieutenant Boger joined the circle around the fire.

"Certainly, friend. And you are right. There will be frost on the blankets when we awake in the morning." Mr. Fritz prided himself on his ability to forcast the coming weather, and was usually accurate.

"Gentlemen, I am Lieutenant Gray Boger, personal aide to General Greene. We have not met, but I believe you may have known my father . . . . "

Before he could complete his sentence, Valentine interrupted. "Ye gads, man, are you Samuel Boger's boy? We bought many a head of cattle from your father, and a finer man never lived in this colony. I am sorry about your recent loss."

"Thank you, sir," Boger replied quietly. "It was quite a blow to my family." Boger's father had been one of the most prosperous cattle traders in the colony, and had drowned the prior spring fording a swollen river with a herd.

"Friends, I have come to greet you, but also because your assistance is sorely needed." Boger had overcome his momentary sadness, and was again all business. "General Greene is planning the details of our northward march, and has asked me to assemble a few loyal gentlemen who know the land north of the Yadkin. I assured him that the three of you could be of assistance."

Valentine replied cautiously. "We are here to help in any way we can, but surely the general has trained scouts who could be of more assistance than we farmers?"

Boger scoffed. "They are either not from here, or

have never gotten down from their horses long enough to look at the lay of the land."

Mr. Fritz laughed. "As our wives would tell you, the three of us have hunted and fished the entire region. We have walked or floated by every inch of land between the Yadkin and the Deep, and know every path, creek and stump. We just never realized we were on a scouting mission."

"Fine, then," said Boger. "Would the three of you be so kind as to join the general for dinner tomorrow evening? He had insisted on making camp among us, but we have prevailed on him to rest comfortably at Mrs. Steele's inn. He will have plenty of nights to sleep out."

When Boger rose to depart, the entire group also stood. "Please tell the general we are honored beyond measure by his request, and will do all we can." Valentine was as astounded as anyone. As Boger disappeared into the dark, the boys all began chortling and slapping each other on the back. "We have only been here a day and already our fathers are meeting with the general to plan the war," said Michael. "I don't plan to sleep tonight. I will wait up for our next guest."

"What in the world are you talking about, Michael? Who else is coming?" Val was completely confused by his brother.

"Oh, I expect by morning to see General Washington himself riding down the road, calling on our fathers to seek their advice." Michael continued to laugh uncontrollably. Thus far, the war had been great fun.

"Settle yourselves, boys, and go to your tents," said Valentine, as he rose to do the same. "Soon enough we will just be farmers again ploughing a furrow."

Chapter 11

The Sabbath

With most of the men away, the group gathered at the church for Sabbath services was small and dispirited. Only the Clodfelter men were present, as they had parted ways with their friends over the war and were determined to stay neutral. They felt that the English King had provided them a safe haven when they fled persecution in Germany, and it was discourteous to now fight against him. Nevertheless, concern for the safety of their neighbors outweighed political differences

"Elizabeth, do you have any meat left in your smokehouse after those rascals raided it?" asked Mr. Clodfelter.

"I'm afraid not, Samuel. We are out, other than the occasional chicken I can pluck. And Philip and Jacob are still too young to go hunting alone. Those two hams were to supply us until Valentine returns and we can slaughter again. But we will get by." Elizabeth was resolute, although more shaken than she would admit from the encounter with the Tories.

"Samuel, this will not do." Matilda Clodfelter was Elizabeth's best friend, and spoke up loudly. "I will not have Elizabeth and her children frightened and hungry while your horrible Tories threaten us all." Although the Clodfelter men were determined to stay neutral in the fighting, Mrs. Clodfelter was decidedly a Patriot.

"Watch your tongue, woman," retorted Mr. Clodfelter. "You are at a house of worship, and they are not *my* Tories or *my* Patriots. I take no side in this conflict."

"Please, my good friends," said Elizabeth. "I wish to cause no discord between you. My children and I will be safe at home. We have arms, and the girls and I can shoot straight. Thank goodness Valentine insisted that we learn."

"Poppycock, Elizabeth. We can do more than that. Were something to happen to you, I could not abide it."

Motioning to her oldest son Reid to approach, Mrs. Clodfelter continued. "Reid, go home and fetch your clothing and rifle, and then ride to the Leonhardts. You will stay there until Mr. Leonhardt returns. And on the next cold day, we will bring over a hog to slaughter and share. I could do with a bit of fresh sausage."

Mr. Clodfelter started to object, but Matilda would have none of it. "Hush, old man. We are doing as I say, or I will take your rifle and go fight with the Patriots."

As Reid quickly mounted his horse to carry out his mother's instructions, Catherine and Barbara looked at each other and giggled. Both liked Reid, and Catherine was particularly sweet on him. Trading their mischievous brothers for Reid was a nice swap. Perhaps this war would not turn out so badly after all.

Mr. Clodfelter spoke loudly. "Now if you ladies are finished organizing our affairs, I suggest we all enter the church and begin services. Prayers must be offered up for those not among us today." And the small band turned and quietly entered the chapel.

Chapter 12

Bad News

Lord Cornwallis stormed at the young man before him as if he were responsible for the bad news he had delivered.

"Tell me again, you idiot, exactly what Colonel Tarleton said," yelled Cornwallis, his face bright red.

"My Lord, I am sorry that I can only repeat what I said earlier. The colonel said to tell His Lordship General Cornwallis that he is defeated, with all but a few of his cavalry taken prisoner by the rebels."

In a desperate attempt to slow the progress of the British army, the Southern army had sent a small force under the command of General Morgan into South Carolina. Their aim was to harass General Cornwallis at every turn, but most importantly, to keep his supplies from Charleston from reaching him. They had been too successful, and General Cornwallis had sent his best commander, Colonel Tarleton, with a cavalry troop to put an end to it. Unbelievably, the rebels had prevailed.

"But how did this happen?" screamed Cornwallis. "Colonel Tarleton commands the best cavalry troop ever to ride under the British flag."

The young man hesitated, unsure if he could safely provide any more information. "He fell into a trap, sir, or so I am told."

"A trap! A trap!" Cornwallis was beside himself. "As if these ragamuffins and half-wits could trap Tarleton. What would you know of a trap, knave?"

The young man paused. "The word was used by Colonel Tarleton, your Lordship. It seems that he came upon a long line of rebel militia in a thin line. They were across an open pasture, where cattle is sold. The local folks call it Cowpens."

For the first time, General Cornwallis was quiet, so the young man continued. "He thought his cavalry could take them easily, and so it appeared. Their militia fired two loads, then ran as if in retreat."

"Exactly so," smiled Cornwallis. "These men are not real soldiers. At the first sign of British soldiers, they turn and run."

"But this time it was a ruse, my Lord. They were not truly retreating. Hiding in the woods was another line of militia, and the first line drew Colonel Tarleton unexpectedly into them. They shot the horses out from under his men, and either killed his men or took them captive. And that is all I know, sir." The lad was obviously relieved to be finished with his mission. He was a young soldier, not used to talking to generals.

The lad started to leave but was called back for one final question. "Where is Tarleton now?" General Cornwallis was already planning his next move.

"He is safe, your Lordship, cautiously making his way back here through the backwoods to avoid capture." As the young soldier exited Cornwallis's tent, he was surprised to feel the general's arm around his shoulder.

"Have some rations, rest, and then report for duty. You have done well." The general as always, had regained his composure when it was time to plan his next move.

The young man walked out of the tent, amazed at the encounter just finished. It is as they say, he thought to himself. Lord Cornwallis is hot-tempered but fair. With a leader like him, they would win this war.

Chapter 13

Ploughing

Barbara had lasted only a single day behind the plough. Although Maude, the family horse, was quite gentle, Barbara had somehow managed to run the plough over her ankle, badly bruising it. She, Mother and Catherine had reached an agreement that Barbara would take over all of Catherine's other chores if she could be excused from the fields. Catherine pretended to be upset, but she was secretly delighted. She much preferred being out in the field to the regular routine of washing, cooking, and cleaning.

The lower field had only been cleared of trees and stumps the year before, and was far from being prime crop land. The plough regularly snagged on tree roots and caught on rocks. Catherine carried the tree roots to a brush pile at the side of the field to be burned later, and piled the rocks up to be used to make walls. Although the work was hard, it was not the monotony of just going round and round in a circle that her brothers complained about.

Reid's arrival had almost upset the arrangement. Elizabeth had assumed that Reid would take over the ploughing, and Catherine would return to her more suitable chores. Catherine had another plan.

"Mother, with all of the men gone, you and Barbara are handling the household chores with little difficulty. But

Reid cannot do the work of four men in the fields. He should join me there, and together we can clear and till the entire field in time for planting." Catherine knew that Mother was usually in favor of any plan that would make the farm more productive.

"Catherine, we only have a single plough horse. Ploughing is not so strenuous that Reid needs you to take a turn with Maude." Elizabeth was interested in the idea only if it would actually work.

"I have thought of that, Mother. We have two ploughs and harnesses. Father purchased a second set of equipment so that a breakdown during planting season would not cause us to lose time."

"What will you use to pull it with, dear?" queried Mother.

"I think Prussia could pull a plough," said Catherine.

"Prussia?" Elizabeth chortled, unable to control her mirth. "Your father would die a thousand deaths if he thought I had harnessed his prize steed to a plough."

Catherine pressed her point. "But he is strong enough to do it, and Reid is strong enough to handle him."

Elizabeth was silent for a moment, and then relented. "We will give it a try, daughter. Everyone else is doing extra work. There is no reason why Prussia should not also."

Although Reid had to use a firm hand with Prussia for the first few days, now they had settled into a comfortable routine. He and Catherine had tried ploughing side by side, but the roughness of the ground meant they were constantly turning rocks or roots into the other's path. So they had hit on a plan to plough in different directions, passing each other each time they circled the field. It was working well.

"We are fortunate that our parents had the courage to flee Germany and settle here," said Reid one morning, as they stopped their work to drink from the pail of water they had brought with them. "It is a good life they have made for us."

"I suppose so," replied Catherine, "if you like farms and cattle."

"And you don't?" asked Reid.

Catherine paused. "I love my family and the life we have on this farm. I just think there must be more."

"What else would you like to do, Catherine?" asked Reid quietly.

"It is not proper to talk such as this, Reid. I should be like Barbara. All she wants in her life is to be exactly like Mother, with a prosperous farm, a good husband, and a tribe of children. She has even picked out the site down the creek where she will build her house. All she needs now is a suitor."

"She will have that soon enough if Thomas Fritz returns from this war," said Reid. He is smitten with Barbara, and just like her, wants to live on this creek bank until he dies. He will just have to gather his courage to ask your Father."

"They would be a good match, Reid, and I will look forward to coming back to visit them and all of my nieces and nephews," giggled Catherine.

"Coming back? Coming back from where?" Reid was perplexed.

Catherine had never talked so freely with anyone about her dreams before, but she felt comfortable with Reid. "I want to live in a town, Reid. I want to live on a crowded street with lots of people, where I can walk out my front door to greet neighbors instead of riding two hours to see a friend."

Reid continued, "But what would you do there?"

Catherine paused and then said, "I will tell you, but you can tell no one. I know it can never happen, but I want to run an inn. I shall call it "Miss Leonhardt's Inn," and it will be well known as a place where a weary traveler can find clean bedding and a good meal. I want to meet people from all over the state, and from even further, and hear their different stories while I provide them lodging and food."

Catherine waited for a response, but Reid was at a loss for words. Disheartened, Catherine said, "I'm sorry I ran on so. Let's get back to work."

"No, wait," said Reid, touching her arm softly. "Do you think a place on this creek bank is all I ever want? Just as you are no Barbara, I am no Thomas Fritz. I have dreams of my own, which I have never dared to tell anyone. And they are not so different from your own."

"What are they?" asked Catherine.

"I want to be a merchant, with a store where farmers from all over the county could bring their crops and trade for the supplies they need. And town folk could come there to buy crops brought by the farmers. I am good with numbers, and know I could do it if I had a chance." Reid's eyes glistened as he talked. Clearly he had given his store as much thought as Catherine had her inn.

They stepped back, each a bit embarrassed at how honestly they had spoken. "We had better go back to our work, Reid," said Catherine. "I will be glad when Father returns. He is not nearly so demanding as Mother."

Chapter 14

Assembling the Troops

Still irritated by the news of Colonel Tarleton's defeat at Cowpens and his unsatisfactory conversation with Governor Martin, General Cornwallis had ordered all of his troops to assemble before him in formation. He addressed them from horseback. "A few miles north of here is a squalid little band of men that calls itself an army," he bellowed, as his horse pranced up and down the line. "They are depraved men of the backwoods, and they have been disloyal to our sovereign King." Pausing for emphasis, he continued. "They must be eradicated, and now is the time." His men roared their support.

"We will move out immediately, and travel quickly. The quartermaster will give each man ten days of rations to carry with him, and enough ammunition for five rounds. Everything else but the ammunition wagons will be burned." Cornwallis's aides looked at each other in astonishment. They had not heard this plan.

"We will trap them against the bank of one of the violent rivers that flow through this godforsaken country, and give them a choice: drown or be shot. Are you with me, men?"

The troops roared their approval. Lord Cornwallis was a battlefield genius, and although his maneuvers were sometimes unusual, they always worked.

"Light the fire, Quartermaster." A small fire had been laid in the middle of the parade ground, and a torch was now put to it. As an example to his troops, Cornwallis rode over to it and tossed his own saddle pouch onto the blaze. Soon all of the soldiers were throwing their own possessions into the fire, anything that would keep them from moving swiftly. Soon, extra supplies and even wagons were thrown on the blaze.

Cornwallis turned to Governor Martin, who was watching with dismay from his coach. He disliked the idea of traveling with the army at all, and now was apparently expected to move at breakneck speed. "Governor, might I suggest that you contribute something as a show of support?" asked the general.

The governor was horrified. He could not imagine undertaking the upcoming march without all of his possessions. "What would you suggest, General?" he responded.

"Why not join us on horseback and send your coach back to New Bern? It would set a fine example for the men to have you at their front." Cornwallis smiled, imagining the discomfort that would be caused the governor were he to make the march on horseback and sleep on the ground.

The governor gathered himself and spoke with full authority. "Ridiculous, General. I am a royal governor, not a common foot soldier. I will travel in my customary style. Do not forget who outranks who here." Having made his position clear, he prepared to leave. "Take me back to my lodging, driver. Send for me, General, when we are to depart."

Chapter 15

The Meeting

"The river is rising quickly. Soon no one will be able to cross it without a boat, even at Trading Ford." As always, Mr. Fritz had an eye on the weather. He and his two friends walked along the muddy path on the south bank of the Yadkin River, from the army encampment outside of town into Salisbury to dine with General Greene.

The Yadkin was one of several rivers that crossed North Carolina from the west to the east. Indian trading paths and colonial roads were located where they could be forded. Each river had shallow spots where, during many months of the year, a wagon, cattle and horses, and even a strong man unafraid of a swift current, could cross. But when they swelled, they became raging torrents that kept any but the bravest from making a crossing. The ferry men that took passengers across on their flat boats would not even attempt it, no matter what fare was offered.

Mr. Klontz chuckled. "Aye, remember the hunting trip several years ago when we camped for a week on this side of the river because we waited too long to cross? And when we did make it home, we all wished we had stayed south of the Yadkin a bit longer."

The three men smiled at the memory. Their wives had been distraught with worry when they were more than a week late returning home, then furious when they realized that they had been loitering on the other side of the river because they had not managed to cross it before it rose. "Even your Elizabeth, Valentine, was irate, and she is a woman of very even temper."

"I recall," grimaced Valentine. "Only an entire bolt of gingham cloth for new dresses returned her to her normal disposition."

The muddy path widened as it entered the town of Salisbury. In less than twenty years, it had grown from only a trading post on the Great Wagon Road to a major town with nearly a hundred buildings. Now there were inns, stores, taverns, tailors, and gun makers. Even lawyers had set up offices, as the county court now sat here regularly.

The three gentlemen approached an attractive two-story white residence on the main street. A small sign at the front door stated: "Inn, Mrs. Steele, Proprietress." As Valentine reached for the brass knocker, the door swung open. A small lady in a lace cap and full gown greeted them with a smile.

"Gentlemen, I am Hanna Steele, and you are most welcome at my inn. We have been expecting you." Behind her stood Lieutenant Boger, who also greeted them warmly.

"Come into the parlour, gentlemen. We will turn to our business, then Mrs. Steele will offer us a fine supper." Boger turned and entered the parlour to the right of the entrance hall, where a large man, plainly dressed with his hair neatly tied back, was intensely studying papers on the table before him.

Not realizing that his visitors had arrived, he spoke to Boger in irritation. "You call these maps? I know more about this countryside from riding through it one time than the imbecile who drew this. Look, here he has the Catawba and Yadkin Rivers almost touching, while my scouts tell me that General Cornwallis is still on the other side of the Catawba more than forty miles away."

"You are right, General." Valentine spoke up. "At no place are those two rivers closer than a day's ride apart."

General Greene looked up with a start. "Good evening, gentlemen. With whom do I have the pleasure of speaking?"

Boger answered. "General, these men are local farmers who have lived in this area for twenty years. They know it well."

"Let's waste no time. Look at this pitiful excuse of a map and draw it for me in a useful way."

The three men quickly moved to the side of the table beside the general and began to peruse the large document before them. After several minutes of study, they began to offer comments.

"As you suggested, General, the Catawba is in the wrong place. It flows much further south, nearer to Charlotte. This map has it passing close to us in Salisbury, but it never flows within fifty miles of this town.

"Good," said the general. "I have ordered General Morgan to leave a regiment of men on this side of the Catawba after he crosses, to prevent General Cornwallis from also crossing. I must have more time to assemble an army. I understand there is only one ford where a crossing is possible."

The three men looked at each other. "Actually, that is not true, General, and all of the local folks know it. Cowan Ford is the site of the public ferry and where most people cross, but there is an unnamed ford four miles up the river where the river is even shallower. You can cross in all but the highest of water." Mr. Fritz spoke hesitantly, in awe of being in the presence of the general.

General Greene turned sharply to Boger. "Does General Morgan know this?"

"I think not, General," replied Boger.

"Then get a messenger to him immediately. He must divide the regiment to forestall the crossing wherever Cornwallis attempts it."

Boger left the room while the conversation continued. "And the river near here, the Yadkin, what can you tell me of it?"

"Its path on the map is accurately drawn," said Mr. Klontz. "But again, the map shows only the main crossing at Trading Ford. There is another equally suitable crossing some ten miles upriver at Indian Ford that is not shown."

"Can this river always be crossed?" said the general.

The men laughed. Valentine said, "We mean no disrespect, General, but from our personal experience, when the Yadkin floods in the late winter, only Jesus walking on water could cross it. You would need to go far upstream to cross."

"How far?" asked the general.

The men looked at each other. "We have never tried it, sir, but I would venture at least fifty miles to get to the shallows in the first mountains." Mr. Klontz spoke, and the other two nodded their agreement.

"And if we go further north on the Great Wagon Road, we come to this river called the Deep. What of it?"

Valentine ventured an answer. "It is a deceptive river, and aptly named. At places it is only fifteen feet wide, but at every spot for fifty miles is more than a man's head deep. You cannot cross it without a boat."

"But this map shows it can be forded easily north of Guilford Courthouse," said the General, pointing to the spot on the map where the ford was shown.

"It can be crossed there, General, but not forded," Valentine continued. There is a wooden bridge there for a crossing. But there is nowhere that it can be forded in that area."

Pointing to the map again, the General added. "Further

north is a river called the Dan. What do you know of it?"
The three friends were perplexed. Why would the general care about a river almost in Virginia? Had he not come to prevent Cornwallis from reaching there? "Now you have left our neighborhood, General," answered Mr. Klontz. I have only seen the Dan River once, when we crossed it on our way from Philadelphia."

"Very well, gentlemen. You have been most helpful, and I am certain I shall seek your advice again as we begin our march." Boger came back into the room.

"Boger, please ask Mrs. Steele to provide these gentlemen with a glass of brandy and some supper. I hope you will excuse me if I do not join you. I have much to do." The gentlemen each shook hands with the general, and moved across the entry hall to the dining room. After they had been served, Mrs. Steele went back into the parlour.

"General, what else may I provide you before I retire for the night?" asked the proprietress.

"Nothing at all, Mrs. Steele, you have been most kind. I arrived here weary and despondent, and your assistance has left me much cheered. Still, I must find provisions for this army, and my pleas to the Continental Congress for funds go unheeded. Perhaps something will arrive on the morrow," said the general as he began to gather his papers to retire for the night.

From the pocket in her apron, Mrs. Steele pulled a cloth purse. "General, this will not do much, but it is all of the gold I have. Take it and use it for the army."

The general was thunderstruck. "Are you certain, madam? If the war is lost, I can never repay you."

"General, I am an old woman. I want to die in a free country. I do not expect repayment." Mrs Steele was insistent.

"I am much cheered, madam. With citizens such as yourself and the gentlemen who were here tonight, you

North Carolinians may have the backbone to see this revolution to an end. But because of the portrait of King George hanging over your mantle, I misjudged you."

Mrs. Steele shrugged. "The judge of the royal court resides with me when court is in session here. It is required."

The general crossed to the fireplace and removed the portrait from the wall. He wrote across the back, "George, you met your end in Mrs. Steele's parlour," and rehung the portrait with the back side showing.

He and Mrs. Stelle laughed. "And on that note I shall retire," said the general.

Waiting a few minutes after he left the room, Mrs. Steele walked to the mantle and righted the King's portrait. An innkeeper never knew who her next guest might be.

Chapter 16

A Sick Child

"Mother, please come quickly." It was well before dawn when Barbara entered her parents's bedroom. "Eliza is very ill."

The two women hurried across the main room to the bedroom the sisters shared. Catherine was holding her little sister, who was moaning softly. "Mother, she woke me to say her throat hurt, and she feels as if she is on fire. Now she can barely speak."

Elizabeth raced to the side of her youngest child and softly touched her forehead. "She is very warm," Elizabeth agreed, trying not to show her alarm. "We may need to send for help."

"But Mother, Reid left today to go home for a few days to help his father clear land. What shall we do?" The worry showed on Barbara's face.

"I will go for help," said Catherine. "I know the way."

"No," said Elizabeth. "The two of you stay here with Eliza." She left the room and climbed the ladder to the loft where now only Jacob and Philip slept. "Jacob, wake up, son."

Jacob sat up, rubbing his eyes. "What is it, Mother?"

"Son, your little sister is very ill, and I am not certain how to treat her. You must go to Mrs. Fritz and ask her to come as quickly as she can."

"What?" asked Jacob. He had never been allowed to go that far, even in the daylight, much less at night.

"Do you remember the path?" asked Elizabeth.

"I am sure I could do it in the daylight, Mother, but I am afraid that I may miss the turn in the dark." Jacob was both excited, and frightened. "But I will try."

"The moon is full and bright tonight; that will help. Dress quickly and fetch Saint from the barn. I will meet you outside to discuss the path you will take." Elizabeth headed back down the ladder to her ailing daughter.

Catherine met her, protesting. "Mother, I can ride for Mrs. Fritz. Jacob is just a little boy."

Elizabeth stood firm. "I will not send daughters out into the night while these evil men are about. A boy will be safer."

Barbara came out of the doorway. "Mother, she is even hotter, and I cannot wake her. What should I do?"

"Continue to wipe her face and arms with cold water to bring down the fever. Pray God Mrs. Fritz has something in that magic chest of hers. Let me go and send Jacob on his way."

Mrs. Fritz was a healer of legendary ability. She had brought her physic chest from Germany, full of herbs and potions. Since arriving in North Carolina, she had expanded her knowledge. She had talked with some of the local Indians about the use of native plants, and even traveled to Salem to converse with the Moravian brothers there about healing methods. She could set a broken bone, stitch up a cut, and cure many aches and fevers. No baby was born without her presence if she could arrive in time. Her presence in the community was a great comfort.

"Jacob, remember to just follow the path on the other side of the creek until you see the large oak tree. Turn there and go along Mr. Fritz's fence line until you reach the house. Stay out of sight and speak to no one. Godspeed, son, and hurry." Elizabeth helped Jacob onto Saint, the gentle old horse on whose back all of the Leonhardt children had learned to ride, and headed back into the house to her youngest.

Jacob found the turn at the oak tree without difficulty, and rode up to the Fritz house. He knocked on the door repeatedly before it opened. Mrs. Fritz stood there in her gown and nightcap.

"Gracious, Jacob, what is a small boy doing here in the middle of the night?" she asked kindly, suspecting the answer.

Jacob quickly explained. Mrs. Fritz disappeared, returning in a few minutes fully dressed, with her chest under her arm. She climbed onto Saint behind Jacob and they headed back to the Leonhardt house.

Elizabeth waited on the porch. She raced to help her friend dismount and gave her a warm embrace. "Sarah, thank you for coming. I am so frightened. I fear it is the quinsy, that killed most of the children in Philadelphia the year we left."

Mrs. Fritz frowned. Quinsy, or diptheria, was the most serious illness a child could face. Few survived it, despite the best treatment. She raced into the house.

"Elizabeth, all of you give me a few minutes to look at her, and we will talk." Mrs. Fritz gently raised Eliza from her pillow, and began to examine her closely. In a few minutes, she came out of the room.

"It is not the quinsy, Elizabeth, but it is very serious. It is the scarlet fever. Her chest and arms are as red as if she has been all day in the summer sun."

Elizabeth sank to her knees. "Sarah, that is as likely to kill her."

"Perhaps," said Mrs. Fritz. "But the scarlet fever we

can fight. There is little I can do if it were quinsy. Barbara, fetch a cold pail of water from the creek. You and Catherine must bathe her all over with wet cloths to bring down the fever. And I will prepare a potion of wormwood as we used in the old country, and the root of coneflower that the Indians use. It helps with the fever. And she must drink, Elizabeth. If she cannot drink from a cup, keep squeezing water from a wet cloth into her mouth."

After the girls left the room, Elizabeth turned to her friend. "I am distraught, Sarah. My husband is away, we are threatened by Tories, my littlest is mortally ill, and so much work on the farm goes undone."

Her friend put her arm around her shoulder. "It is a hard time for all of us, Elizabeth, and is always hardest right before the dawn. It will be better once your little girl is out of danger."

For two days, the Leonhardt women did little but tend to their youngest. Mrs. Fritz came daily to examine her and give her a potion. On the third morning, Elizabeth was awakened from an exhausted sleep by someone pulling on her sleeve. It was Eliza, her fever broken.

"Excuse me, Mother," said the little girl, "but I am exceedingly hungry. When may we have breakfast?"

Elizabeth laughed aloud, hugged her smallest daughter, and carried her down the stairs to the kitchen. "Right now, little one. I will make your favorite griddle cakes."

Chapter 17

Making an Example

Reviewing his troops the next day after the meeting at Mrs. Steele's inn, General Greene was distraught. He turned to Boger, and said, "It is even worse than it seemed yesterday. Many of these men have only rags tied on their feet, and some little more than blankets tied around their waists for clothing."

Boger nodded. "The Continental Congress has repeatedly promised us provisions, but none ever come. But the purse of gold you gave me this morning will help. Already local tanners are making boots for our men."

General Greene continued to look over the grounds where the army was camped. "And there seem to be even fewer men here today than there were yesterday. Are some off on maneuvers?"

Boger responded. "No, General, many live in the area, and go and come as they please."

"What?" shouted the general. "How long has this been happening?"

Boger shrugged. "As long as I have been with the army. General Gates was never very concerned, so long as the men were present when he was ready to march or fight."

The general was lost in thought. "Review for me the terms under which the militia joins the army, Boger."

"It is the same here as everywhere, sir. The commitment is for six months, except for the older men, who must only stay sixty days." Boger was unsure why the general was asking these questions.

"And you are sure that every man understands that this is his legal obligation when he joins?" queried the general.

"It is read to all when they enlist, sir, and each signs his name or makes his mark on the roll."

"Fine. Bring me the first man who returns who has been away without a furlough. I wish to talk to him."

Later that evening, a young farmer from an adjoining farm was brought to Greene's tent. The general was pleasant. "Tell me your name, private?"

The tongue-tied young man answered, "Schmidt, sir."

"Private Schmidt, you joined the army for six months, did you not?"

"Yessir."

"And where have you been for the last two days, son?"

"I went back to my father's farm, general. There is a young lady near there who I hope to marry, and I was afraid that if she did not see me for six months, she would marry another. But I come back."

"And did your lieutenant give you permission to take leave?" continued General Greene.

"No sir, but I didn't figure he would mind if I come back."

"That's all, private. You may go."

As the young man left, the general turned to Boger. "Assemble the entire army for a general muster. There is a lesson to be taught."

Less than an hour later, the entire Army of the South was assembled in formation, their first before their new commanding officer. General Greene strode before them.

"Soldiers, we are facing a perilous time. Lord

Cornwallis is only a few miles south of us, and threatens to attack at any minute. If he prevails, our entire cause will be lost. And yet I find an army in which discipline is lax, and morale is poor. Private Schmidt, step forward."

The befuddled young man stepped to the front of the ranks.

"Private, you are accused of desertion. You admitted to me that you left the army two days ago without permission. Guards, seize him." A platoon of soldiers stepped forward to do the general's biding.

Boger was aghast. He saw what was about to happen, and feared his new commander misunderstood the proud North Carolinians before him. There would be a mutiny.

"Guards, take Private Schmidt to yonder tree, tie him to it, and give him ten lashes. The penalty for desertion is death, but today I will be merciful." The young man began to whimper, and other soldiers began to murmur in protest.

General Greene drew his pistol. "The first man who breaks rank will die by my hand. We will either fight as a proper army, or we will die under the heel of the British king. Do as I commanded."

Without more ado, Schmidt was dragged to the nearest tree and the sentence carried out. General Greene dismissed the troops, and much to Boger's relief, the army returned to their campsites. As one grizzled veteran passed by him, Boger heard him remark, "Ye gods, men, the new general is a proper soldier. Now we are in a real army." Once again, Boger was in awe of his new commander.

Chapter 18

River Crossing

"There is no need for a sentry tonight," said General Meade, sighing with relief as he looked at the rising water of the swollen Catawba River below him. "Today was Cornwallis's last opportunity to cross before the spring floods. God has provided General Greene with some time to build his army." General Meade and his aides turned and headed to their camp in a high spot a few hundred yards off the north bank of the river.

On the south side of the river, Cornwallis was slightly less than a mile from the ford. Pausing in his march, he was engaged in a vigorous discussion with his aides. "Your Lordship," said his senior aide, "the river is rising quickly. It is doubtful that our men can walk across, and certainly our ammunition wagons will be flooded."

Cornwallis would not be dissuaded. "We cross tonight, after midnight when least expected. Tell each man to carry his ammunition in his hat. The wagons will come later when the river recedes. If we cross here tonight, then Greene and his misfits will be trapped on this side of the Yadkin River and we can finish them off. I am tired of this pestilent colony. We will end it soon and be back in England for the summer."

Governor Martin was listening nearby. "General," he said, "I will wait here with the ammunition wagons. I cannot risk my coach in such conditions."

"Nonsense," smiled Cornwallis. "I am sure your strong steeds will have no difficulty with the current, and my men need your constant encouragement." Governor Martin was silent, once again bested by the general.

Several hours later, the British army approached the raging river in silence. "This is foolishness," whispered Governor Martin. "Men cannot be expected to walk through this torrent."

Cornwallis paid him no mind. Driving his horse into the water, he commanded his men to follow. They did so without question.

It was trickier going than even the general expected. The river bottom was slippery underneath, and numbers of men lost their footing and were swept downstream. Above the din came a girlish scream, as Governor Martin's horses lost their footing and his coach began to float. It was enough to arouse the troops on the other side. As they raced to the river, they were amazed to see the first wave of British soldiers emerge on the north bank. As if just completing a summer swim, they assembled into formation, pulled dry powder from under their hats and begin to fire.

The rebels panicked and ran. The British soldiers were unlike any other foe they had ever met. Now on the north bank, Cornwallis assembled his aides. "We have lost at least a score of men that were swept downstream, General, but everyone else is across safely," said his senior aide.

"What of our fine governor?" smiled Cornwallis.

"His horses regained their footing, and pulled his coach ashore some yards downstream. He is shaken but fine."

"That is good news. We would be lost without him," said Cornwallis, chuckling with all of his aides. "Now we head to Salisbury and finish this."

Chapter 19

Race to Virginia

"I have never been this cold," said Val, shivering as he huddled under a blanket with his brothers as an icy rain fell. The army had been on the march all day and into the night, stopping only to eat dry corn meal and jerky. Morale was low. For three weeks, the army had fled northward across North Carolina, only a step in front of Cornwallis's larger force. They had plunged into the icy waters of the Yadkin River at Trading Ford in the middle of the night when word came that Cornwallis had crossed the Catawba. The waters were too high for even Cornwallis to cross when he reached Trading Ford the next day, but he quickly marched his men fifty miles upstream, crossed, and continued the pursuit. Greene thought they had escaped him when they crossed the only bridge on the Deep River and then destroyed it, but somehow the wily general had commandeered enough boats from local Tories to float his troops across. Now he was close on their heels again.

"I don't understand what we are doing," muttered Michael. "I thought we joined the army to keep Cornwallis from getting to Virginia, and now we are leading him there. Will we never just stand and fight him?"

As usual, Peter had an answer. Again, he had been listening to the older men talk. "Although we and our friends joined the militia, not enough of our fellow North

59

Carolinians answered the call. We are still too few to defeat the British. If we fight now, it will be over or so says Father."

"So we run like rabbits from the hound," sneered Michael. "If this is war, even I will take to the life of a farmer."

The boys were interrupted by Lieutenant Boger coming down the line of troops on his steed. "On your feet, men. The Dan River is only a few miles in front of us. With any speed, we will be there at dawn. Make haste. Cornwallis is so close we can see his campfires in the distance behind us."

The brothers joined the weary march on the muddy path north. The army had given up any semblance of a marching formation. Each man simply trudged along in the numbing cold, staying on his feet as best he could. The boots of many had soles so worn through that bloody footprints could be seen on the frozen ground.

Several hours later, as dawn was breaking, the path widened and the Dan River came into sight. Along its banks was lined a flotilla of boats of all shapes and sizes. Valentine, Mr. Klontz and Mr. Fritz stood among the boats, talking to General Greene.

"Are you sure, gentlemen?" asked the general.

Valentine answered quickly. "Sir, we have spent several days up and down this river, and there is no place within thirty miles that it can be crossed without a boat."

"And are you certain that these are all of the boats in this area? I do not want to be surprised again to see Cornwallis floating after me as he did at the Deep River."

Again, Valentine spoke. "General, few people live along this river, and we have gone with your troops to every house and bought or taken every boat of any kind. He will cross on floating logs if he crosses at all."

As the men spoke, the cannons were lashed onto the

largest boats, and the supply wagons unloaded onto others. "Climb on, men. The Dan River ferry is open for business." As usual, Lieutenant Boger was moving the troops along.

"Let's go, brothers," shouted Michael, and the three raced for a dugout canoe pulled onto the bank. Peter grabbed the paddle, and began the quick trip across. On the other side, Michael and Val quickly jumped out, while Peter rowed back across for more passengers. In this fashion, the entire army was across the river by mid-morning.

As the army started to march into Virginia, Valentine suddenly asked Boger for a word with the general. His request granted, Valentine made his point. "General, we must take the boats with us, or destroy them. Otherwise, one brave British soldier could swim the river, bring the first boat back, and in short order have the entire British army across."

The general thought for a moment. "We cannot destroy them, sir, or we will be trapped in Virginia ourselves. Boger, burn the boats that are too heavy to carry, and take the lighter ones with us. Hopefully, we will need them soon."

As General Greene and Lieutenant Boger stood in the safety of the north bank of the Dan, they heard the fife and drum of Cornwallis approaching the other bank. "Are we really free of him for a bit, General?" asked Boger.

"I think so," said General Greene. "He cannot get across, and he has outrun his supplies. And there are few people in this area to take them from. He will be forced to retreat."

"What are we to do here in Virginia, sir?" asked Boger.

"It is very simple, Boger. Either the Virginians will heed our call and come to our aid, or it is over. We shall know in a few days."

Chapter 20

The Battle

"God protect us," murmured Mr. Klontz, as he looked at the field below him. From out of the woods came row upon row of British troops, marching in perfect order to fife and drum. Their bayonets and gold epaulets glistened in the sun.

The Great Wagon Road came up a small hill through an open field to Guilford Courthouse. General Greene had positioned his army in three rows near the top. The first line was the North Carolina militia, now a thousand men stretched out in a single line across the hillside.

The Leonhardts, Fritzes, and Klontzes were all side by side on the left flank. The older men had debated this placement, whether it was better to disperse through the line or stay together. In the end, they had determined to remain as one.

General Greene rode down the line on horseback. "Men of Carolina, remember that you fight today for your farms, your families, and your freedom. Your task is simple. Hold your fire until the British are in range. Fire two rounds, and fall back." The men nodded. It seemed simple enough.

"I am frightened, Michael," said Val to his older brother beside him.

Michael laughed. "So is everyone, Val. We are all trying not to wet ourselves. Just pick out two men in red
coats, fire at them, and move back. We'll be fine."

As the British continued their steady march up the hill,
Lieutenant Boger rode up and down, cautioning the troops.
"Steady, men, steady. Hold fire until they are in range."
Although the men on the left flank did as instructed, the
militia on the right flank panicked. First one rifle sounded,
then another, and soon everyone on that side of the road
was firing. Unfortunately, the British were still out of range,
so the round was useless.

"Damnation!" shouted Boger. "Hold your fire on this
side, I say."

The nervous men did as they were told, although it
seemed that the British were practically on top of them.
Finally, the order to fire came. Peter and Val shouted with
glee as they watched the British soldiers in their sights
topple backwards. As nonchalantly as if out for a walk in
Hyde Park, the British line reformed and continued up the
hill.

On the right side, all was chaos. A number of the
militiamen, terrified that their first round had not slowed the
British at all, had turned and run. Their officers on horseback, with curses and threats, were trying to stem the
flight, but with little success. As the entire British army
swung to the left to take advantage of the opening, the
men on the left flank calmly fired their second round, and
began to move back. The older men looked down the line
and realized with relief that their sons were all safe.

Now the British army faced the Virginia militia in the
second line. These were the troops who had come to
General Greene's assistance while he was camped on the
north side of the Dan River. They had given him confi-
dence to come back south into North Carolina and finally
battle Cornwallis. They held firmer than the North Caro-

lina militia on the right flank, firing two deadly rounds and then retreating as instructed. Now the British army faced General Greene's third line and most experienced troops, the Maryland Regulars. The two lines fired at each other, and then the British charged with their bayonets. The Maryland troops stood their ground, and soon the two armies were locked in hand-to-hand combat.

"Father, we must help them," shouted Michael, from the hill above where the North Carolina militia had retreated.

"Stay here, son, as we have been ordered. Our turn will come again," replied Father, sternly.

Thomas Fritz spoke up. "Not if they are all killed with British bayonets, and only because our North Carolina boys turned and ran. Come on, Michael." Despite their father's orders to turn back, the two raced toward the battle. After a moment's hesitation, the other young men followed.

Suddenly Boger appeared on horseback. "Gentlemen," he said. "The general has need of you. We are running out of ammunition, and he needs your knowledge of the land to plan a safe retreat." Moving quickly, the men raced up the hill after Boger toward General Greene's tent.

From below, Lord Cornwallis watched the hand-to-hand combat with mounting alarm. To his surprise, the Continental troops were not retreating, and with their superior numbers, they threatened to destroy his entire army. He called to his aide, "Load the cannon with grapeshot, and fire it into the fight."

His aide was horrified. "But we will hit our troops as well as the continentals, General."

"It cannot be helped," replied Cornwallis cooly. "Do as I say or all will be lost."

At General Greene's tent, the three men were again bent over a map with the General. Valentine finally spoke. "General, there is a cartway along Little Horsepen Creek on the back side of this hill firm enough for wagons. About five miles downstream, it widens into a pleasant meadow that would be easy to defend. The woods here are nearly impassable except for the path along the creek.

As the two friends nodded agreement, the conversation was interrupted by the roar of cannons and the screams of dozens of men. "He is a maniac," yelled Boger. "He has fired into his own troops."

"Unfortunately, he is a brilliant maniac," replied General Greene. "He is betting that his experienced troops can now reform faster than we can, and he is likely right. We are out of ammunition, Boger. Sound the retreat."

General Greene turned to the three friends. "Your advice has been invaluable, gentlemen. You are free to return to your farms and families. There will be no more battles during your sixty-day commitment. But you must leave me your fine sons."

Valentine, stunned by the carnage he had just witnessed below him, replied, "We will, General. All that survived Cornwallis's brutality."

General Greene looked back over his shoulder as he strode off. "Take any with you that are too injured to fight, but leave me the rest. Good day, gentlemen."

The three friends returned to the hill where they had last seen their sons, not knowing how else to locate them. As the bugle sounded retreat and they were ordered to move out, suddenly from the dust came the group of young men. At first they all looked fine, but then they realized that Michael was being supported by his brothers, and his shirt was bright red.

"He took a bayonet in the shoulder, and is bleeding badly," yelled Peter. Valentine raced to examine the wound.

"Where is Thomas?" asked Mr. Fritz sharply.

"We can't find him, sir," said Val. "We were separated in the fight, and the cannon fire threw everything into confusion."

Mr. Fritz started racing down the hill toward the battle, but was stopped by his friends. "Do not be foolish, my friend," said Valentine. "Soon there will be a flag of truce for each side to claim its wounded and dead. Do not get yourself killed for naught. We will not leave without your boy."

Chapter 21

Thomas's Ordeal

Thomas's last recollection was the loud roar of a cannon before he felt as if his right leg had been removed from his body. At first the pain was intense, then it receded. As night came, he began to think of how pleasant home would be at suppertime, and wished he had not been so frightened to ask Barbara to marry him before he left. All around him, men lay moaning and weeping.

A group of men carrying a white flag approached him and turned him over roughly. "Put him on the wagon. If we take off that leg soon, he has a chance of surviving." Two young soldiers picked him up and laid him on the floor of the wagon, and the group continued to move through the field. Some men they ignored, while others were added to the wagon bed. Thomas writhed in pain until it became so intense he lost consciousness.

When he awoke, he was laying outside a farmhouse on the ground. Rows of men were nearby, and from inside the house they could hear screaming. Suddenly, the two young soldiers who had loaded him onto the wagon were at his side. "The Captain says to take him next, if he's to have any chance at all."

Thomas was carried into the farmhouse and laid on the kitchen table. The leg of his pants was cut away, exposing the raw wound where the grapeshot had entered. An older man, wrapped in a bloody apron and holding a saw, looked at it quickly. "Hold him tight, boys. I will take it off midway between his waist and knee."

Thomas screamed with horror as he realized what was about to happen. If he lived, he would be crippled for the rest of his life. "Wait, please, do not do this," he sobbed uncontrollably.

"Hold him, boys," said the surgeon, as he marked the spot to begin to cut.

From the doorway came a sharp voice. "Touch my boy with that saw and it will be the last cut you ever make." It was Mr. Fritz, with Valentine and Mr. Klontz close behind.

The surgeon held his ground. "Your son is a dead man if I do not cut. His thigh is bloodied by grapeshot and the bone is broken."

Mr. Fritz moved to the table and picked up Thomas in his arms. "It will not be on your head, sir, but on mine. I am taking him home. His mother is a healer. She has saved many a broken limb."

The surgeon sneered. "Take him away, then. But the only thing his mother will do is go to his funeral."

With Mr. Fritz carrying Thomas, the three men went out of the farmhouse to the yard where their other sons were waiting. Michael was already tied on a horse they had captured from the battlefield.

"Tie Thomas on behind Michael, boys, and tightly so that they do not slide off," said Mr. Fritz. After briefly embracing the sons they were leaving with the army, the three friends started for home with their wounded boys.

Chapter 22

Encounter in the Woods

"Father, please, could I have another sip," begged Thomas. He was in sharp pain from the leg wound and the whiskey in his father's knapsack was the only medicine available.

"Just a drop more, son," said Mr. Fritz, pouring a small amount into a cup and handing it to Thomas. He was worried. His son was clearly in agony, and the wound was beginning to fester.

"How much longer, Valentine?" queried Mr. Fritz. The men had walked all of the prior day from Guilford Courthouse, leading the horse carrying their wounded sons.

"If the boys can stay on the horse, we can be home by nightfall," responded Valentine. "I believe Michael can make it, but we may have to stop for Thomas to rest."

A noise in a clearing ahead of them caught their attention. "What do you hear?" asked Mr. Klontz. "It sounds like men arguing."

"The two of you stay back with the boys and cover me while I walk ahead," said Valentine. Before the war, the men would have gone on and greeted whoever they met. But these were perilous times, and caution was required.

An alarming sight greeted Valentine as he entered the clearing. On horseback was a terrified young man, scarcely older than Thomas or Michael. A rope tied to a sturdy limb above him ended in a noose around his neck. His hands were tied behind his back. Three men on foot were taunting him.

"So, you little rebel, is it a family you are heading home to?" The smallest of the three men was clearly in charge, dressed in the coat of a British dragoon and wearing a peculiar silk cap.

"Please, sir, I mean no harm. Just let me go home to my wife and son." The young man's voice trembled with fright.

The small man sneered. "You will never see them again on this earth. Perhaps in Heaven." As he picked up a stick to strike the horse, Valentine stepped into the clearing.

"Good day, gentlemen. Caught a murderer or horse thief, I see. It's best to hang them quickly, don't you agree?" Valentine continued to approach where the men were standing. "And to whom do I have the honor of speaking?"

"Colonel David Fanning of the royal militia, as if it is any of your business, old farmer. This man is worse than a thief or murderer. We caught him sneaking home from fighting for the rebels at Guilford Courthouse. He is being hanged for disloyalty to his king. Now be about your business and leave us to ours." He again raised the stick to strike the horse.

"One minute, Colonel," responded Valentine. "I did not realize that the British hang soldiers. Should you not do the honorable thing and take this man as a prisoner of war?"

Exasperated, Colonel Fanning responded. "Enough, old man, or you will be next. Now be off."

Valentine raised his musket and pointed it at Colonel Fanning. "Cut him down and send him on his way. He has committed no crime."

Colonel Fanning laughed. "So with your old musket you can take the three of us?"

Mr. Klontz and Mr. Fritz stepped from the bushes, their muskets drawn also. Valentine smiled. "By my count it will take three bullets, and coincidentally, that is what we have. Now cut him down."

Fanning nodded to one of his henchmen, who untied the boy's hands and removed the noose from around his neck. The boy climbed off the horse.

"What is your name, boy?" asked Valentine.

"Samuel, sir, Samuel Hege. And you, sir?" Even under the stress of almost being hung, the young man still recalled his manners.

"I am Valentine Leonhardt, and these are my good friends, Frederick Fritz and Ralph Klontz. We were also with General Greene at Guilford Courthouse, together with our sons, and are also headed home."

"I am glad you took this path today, sir," smiled Samuel.

Valentine looked at the three Tories before him. "Let me ask you something, Samuel. Could your family do with some horses?"

"Yes, sir. Ours were taken by the Tories. That is why I decided to go to fight."

"Then I suggest you take home the three these gentlemen were riding. It is not theft to steal from thieves."

As Samuel began to tie the horses together, Valentine continued. "How about some rifles? Could your family use three good Tory rifles?"

Samuel smiled, and picked up the three rifles from the ground where Colonel Fanning and his men had laid them while preparing to hang him. Now Samuel was eager to leave.

"Before you go, Samuel, how about some boots? These men all seem to have fine ones." Valentine, Mr. Klontz and

Mr. Fritz were now all laughing. "Take them off, gentlemen, and hand them to Samuel." The Tories hesitated, until Valentine cocked his weapon. "Do as I say, or you will die in this lonely spot." Reluctantly, the three men took off their shoes.

"And one more thing, Samuel. It is a bitterly cold day, and you have no coat. Colonel Fanning, please give him yours." Fanning glowered with hatred as he handed over his prized coat.

"And as I look further, Samuel is not wearing proper britches for riding. Take off your leather chaps also, and hand them to him." Even Colonel Fanning's two henchmen could not hide a smile as he removed his pants and stood before the group barefooted, in just his longjohns and silk cap.

"Samuel, do you have any need for longjohns?" laughed Valentine.

"No sir, mine are fine. And if I may take my leave, I'll be headed for home." Samuel left, now with three horses, three rifles, and a new outfit.

Valentine turned to an enraged Colonel Fanning. "We will also take our leave now, gentlemen. It was a pleasure meeting you. Good day."

Mr. Klontz spoke up. "Valentine, shouldn't we just shoot them as we do other vermin?"

"Leave them be, Ralph." Valentine began to walk back toward the horse where Michael and Thomas were waiting. "We are God-fearing North Carolinians, not Tory pagans. Let's get our boys home to their mothers."

Chapter 23

Homecoming

"Take him off gently, friends," said Mr. Fritz. The last few hours of the journey home had been so difficult for Thomas that he had fainted from pain. Only by leaning on Michael's back was he able to stay on the horse. Mrs. Fritz and the younger children came running from the house.

"Mother, our boy is gravely wounded. He needs you."

Mrs. Fritz nodded and took charge. "Take him into the bedroom and cut away his trousers. Daughters, fetch me hot water, clean cloth, and my medicine chest." She turned to Valentine. "And what of Michael?"

"He took a bayonet through the shoulder, but it seems to have gone through cleanly. He can move his arm, so no bone is broken. Tend to Thomas first and we will wait," he replied.

Nodding, she hurried into the house to begin her preparations. After Thomas was stretched out on the bed, she began her examination. Although she gasped at her first look, upon closer examination it was not as bad as she feared. The grapeshot had torn a nasty gash in his upper thigh, but she could feel no metal left in the wound. His thigh bone was broken above the knee, but more likely from the fall than the grapeshot. Although it was out of place, it had not protruded through the skin. She was heartened. He had a chance of surviving.   She called for her husband and Mr. Klontz

"Come in here quickly, and do as I say. His thigh bone must be set in place or he will never walk again. Husband, grab his waist, and Ralph, below his knee. When you pull, I will rotate the bone. Do not stop when he screams."

When everyone was in position, Mrs. Fritz shouted, "Now." Thomas regained consciousness with the most painful scream anyone had ever heard, but his mother continued twisting his leg until she was satisfied the bone was back in place. "Stop now. The ends are touching, and it has a chance to heal." She reached in her chest, took out a pinch of white powder, and put it under her son's tongue. "This powder of opium will dull his pain. Let me bandage Michael's shoulder and send him home to his mother, and then I will come back and splint the leg and stitch the wound together."

As Mrs. Fritz rushed out of the room to tend to Michael, Mr. Klontz, still shaken from his part in setting Thomas's leg, smiled weakly at his friend. "Your wife is a remarkable woman, Frederick. We are fortunate to have her among us."

"She is that, friend. But if I am ever hurt this badly, promise that you will just shoot me. I do not believe I could stand what my son has for these past two days. And now you should head to your home so your family will know that you are safe." As Mr. Klontz departed, Mr. Fritz sat quietly on the bed, gently stroking his sleeping son's head.

Chapter 24

Fanning's Revenge

The messenger arrived at Colonel Fanning's hideout in a remote forest near the Deep River. With the departure of the British from the area, sentiment had swung heavily in favor of the rebels. The colonel and his men could only move with great stealth. The messenger came straight from Governor Martin, having ridden for two days.

"Colonel, the news is disastrous. Lord Cornwallis has surrendered, and his entire army taken prisoner. It is over."

Fanning was astounded. "How could that be? His troops are the finest in Britain, and since the victory at Guilford Courthouse have not even been attacked."

"It was the French," said the messenger. "Their fleet finally came to the aid of the rebels. His Lordship was caught in Virginia, at a place called Yorktown, trapped against the ocean and unable to escape to the British fleet. Governor Martin has sent me to tell you that you are not safe."

Fanning scoffed, "As if I didn't already know that."

"But it is worse, Colonel," the messenger continued. "The rebel governor has issued a proclamation forgiving all Tories who fought for the British, and allowing them to keep their land and possessions. And for those who desire to leave, he has granted safe passage away from the colony on British ships now off the coast of Wilmington."

"But that is all good news," said Fanning. "All is forgiven. What fools," he said, smiling.

"There are exceptions, sir, from the proclamation. Three men are named who will never be forgiven. If seen, they are to be shot on sight, or hanged immediately. You are one of the three. The governor says to make your way to Wilmington by stealth and disguise, and he will assist you in boarding a British ship."

"What of my men?" asked Fanning.

"They are not named," said the messenger. "They are free to return home."

Fanning turned to the two men who had stayed by his side the entire war. "Well, boys, this is where we part ways. But I would ask one more thing of you before you leave."

One of his henchmen, who rarely spoke, anticipated what he thought the colonel would say. "Do not worry, colonel, we will gather your wife and children and bring them to you at Wilmington."

Fanning shook his head. "No, it is not that. There is no time to fetch them. They will have to fend for themselves until I can send for them. It is another matter."

His men, surprised, stood waiting. "There are some haughty German farmers nearby, one with an overly proud wife, who need to be taught a final lesson before we leave."

His men protested. "It will take too much time, Colonel, and you will miss your boat. Besides, the fighting is over."

"We will harm no one, fellows, only burn a barn or two. Just a reminder that you cannot make a fool of Fanning and suffer no consequences." Colonel Fanning had never recovered from the humiliation of being left barefoot in his underwear. It did not help that he was derisively known now by the local citizens as "Longjohn Fanning."

"It is risky, sir. These men are good soldiers, and each has two or three strong sons home from the war." His supporters, always loyal, were wavering.

"Come on, lads. One more bit of fun before we go our separate ways. Unless a lucky shot comes my way, we will be content with burning their barns. Their crops are just in. They will remember me during the hard winter when they are hungry."

The men agreed. "But one more night of amusement, and then we will bid you goodbye." The men mounted their horses and left their hideout for the last time.

Chapter 25

Tragedy

Valentine stepped out of the privy, and headed toward the house. On the front porch, Philip and Jacob were playing marbles. "Up the stairs to bed, boys. We will get an early start in the morning." Father had promised to take his youngest sons on a fishing trip. With the harvest in, everyone was taking advantage of free time and the unseasonably mild November weather. Now that Michael and Thomas Fritz were fully healed, his older sons and their friends had gone on a hunting expedition.

Valentine entered the main room, where Elizabeth was knitting in her chair by the hearth. He patted her on the shoulder, then went to sit in his chair. As he lit his pipe, he said, "It is good to be back in calm waters, is it not, Mother?"

She smiled without replying. Each knew how hard the previous year had been.

"I shall head to bed now, Husband," said Elizabeth. "While our older sons are hunting, and you and our younger sons are off fishing, your daughters and I are to spend the day making candles." She pretended to be stern, but Valentine knew she loved nothing better than to spend a day without interruption in a household project.

As she moved to bolt the door, Valentine said, "Leave

it. The cool air is pleasant this evening. I will shut the top
and bolt it when I come in." Mother patted him on the
top of the head as she passed, and headed into their room.

Valentine sat by the hearth, enjoying the last embers of
his pipe. His mind ran to the hardships his family had
endured during the past year, and how fortunately matters
had turned out. Eliza had survived the scarlet fever, Michael
had recovered from his bayonet wound, and his fearless
wife had prevented Catherine from being harmed. Now, his
daughters were betrothed to two fine young men, and with
a final trip to Salisbury the future of his older sons would
be assured. He was indeed a lucky man. As he mused,
the weariness of the day overtook him and he dozed.

Although he had gone to bed as Father had ordered,
a sudden pain in Jacob's stomach suggested he should
relieve himself before sleeping. He quietly crept down the
attic ladder, and smiled at his father snoring in his chair
by the hearth. He headed out into the night and crossed
the yard to the family privy. From inside, he thought he
heard the sound of horses on the path to the house, but
then they stopped. In his dreams inside the house, Valentine also heard horses approaching.

As the boy came out of the privy, a gunshot shattered
the silence. He raced toward the house in time to see a
small man carrying a rifle jump off of the porch and race
down the path away from the house. Out of the darkness,
two more running men joined him. He heard them mount
horses and race away.

Frightened, Jacob raced toward the house. Mother was
kneeling beside Valentine's body on the floor, wiping blood
from his head with her nightgown. She spoke sharply. "Barbara, Catherine, bring hot water and cloth for bandages.
Father is badly wounded." As his sisters came running from
their room, Jacob heard a familiar whinny and raced to the
door. Flames were coming from the roof of the barn, and

Saint and the other horses were trapped inside.

"Mother, the barn is on fire," yelled Jacob, as he took off running.

"Do not leave this house. There are murderers about, and there is little you can do." He usually obeyed his mother without question, but this time he ignored her as he ran across the barnyard. The latch on the barn door was secured, but Jacob beat it loose with a piece of wood he found nearby. He opened the door and called.

"Saint, come here, boy. Come here." Terrified of the fire, Saint, Prussia, Maude and the other horses refused to move, whinnying and bucking in place.

Jacob raced in, and leaped on Saint's back. The entire roof of the barn was on fire, and the horses were paralyzed by fright. "Come on, Saint," he said, kicking the animal furiously. But still he would not budge.

Remembering how his father tricked horses afraid of bonfires used to clear fields, he jerked off his nightshirt and pulled it over Saint's head to hide the fire. Now when Jacob kicked him, the horse responded. Saint raced out of the barn, with the other horses following, just as the burning roof collapsed. Jacob jumped off and led him to the creek where he and the other horses, still quivering from fright, took a long drink.

Catherine ran frantically aound the yard, screaming. "Mother, I cannot find Jacob, and the barn has just fallen in from the fire."

"Over here, Catherine, by the creek," shouted Jacob. "I am fine."

She raced to him and gave him a tight hug. "But Jacob, why do you have no clothes on? Were they burned?" He explained how he had persuaded the horses to flee the burning barn, as he took his nightshirt from around Saint's neck and slipped it over his head.

"It was him, Catherine. I saw him in the moonlight."

"Who?" asked Catherine, not comprehending.

"It was that horrible little Tory man who threatened you. He shot Father. I saw him jump off the porch with his rifle."

Catherine took a deep breath. "Are you sure?"

"I am," said Jacob. "He had on that same silly cap."

"Is Father . . . ?" asked Jacob softly. He could not bear to say the words.

"No, but he is badly hurt. Hurry, we must show Mother that you are fine. At least that is one thing that will not worry her." They raced to the house.

Chapter 26

A Sad Return

After three days in the woods, the young men were in a festive mood as they headed home. Their pack horses were laden with deer and wild turkeys that their mothers would cure and store in smokehouses for the winter.

"This will most likely be your last hunting trip, Thomas," joked Michael. "Our sister Barbara will be a hard wife. She will have you ploughing day and night."

"And poor Reid," added Peter. "You will be so busy emptying chamber pots at Catherine's inn you will forget what the outdoors looks like."

Thomas and Reid took playful swipes at the Leonhardt brothers, but knew the jesting was all in fun. The brothers were delighted that their sisters were marrying their friends.

Just as they reached the turnoff to the Fritz house, a rider came barreling down the road at full gallop. "I say, lads," said the man, pausing only slightly. "Are ye Patriots or godforsaken Tories?"

"Patriots all," replied Peter.

"Then ye shall like the news I am racing to Salisbury to tell. The fighting is over. Cornwallis and all of his bloody troops have surrendered, gotten back on their ships, and sailed back to their bloody King George. We are a free people."

The young men were stood speechless. Finally, Val asked, "Are you certain, sir?"

"That I am, young man. I have the official proclamation from our free governor in my saddlebag. It gives all Tories who wish to leave the colony safe passage to Wilmington to board the last British ships leaving the harbor." Returning to his gallop, he was soon out of sight.

The young men broke into a jog, eager to tell their fathers the good news. First the Fritz boys turned off to their house, and then the Klontzes. Before long, the Leonhardt brothers were racing down the path to their home. They raced up the steps in unison, shouting, "Father, Mother, it is over, we have won . . . . " Suddenly they were brought up short by the tearful and grieving faces of their mother and sisters.

"Quiet, sons, this is no time for shouting," said Mother. "You have returned to a very sad house. Your father was shot in the head last night through the open door as he sat in his chair by the fire."

The boys were stunned. "Is he . . . ?" mumbled Val, unable to say the word.

"No, he still lives, but he is unconscious. He is in his bed, and thankfully, seems in no pain."

Peter spoke next. "Mother, what happened?"

Elizabeth recounted the events of the prior evening, trying to compose herself as she spoke. "And we know who shot your father, boys. Jacob saw him. It was that miserable little man who took our gold and hams and threatened Catherine."

"Fanning," said Michael, spitting out the name as he started up the stairs to the sleeping loft. "Let us pack our bags, Mother, and we will chase him to the gates of Hell before he gets away with this." Peter and Val started to follow.

"You will not, my sons." Elizabeth now spoke firmly.

"You are needed here. Mrs. Fritz was just here, and her diagnosis was grim. Your father is mortally wounded, and cannot recover. And the news is even worse. Mr. Klontz was also shot last night, and did not survive until morning."

The boys stood silent, then protested. "But Mother, we cannot let him escape after these vile deeds."

Elizabeth remained firm. "Do you not think that if we could catch the little weasel, I would not ride myself? But he has a day's head start, and if you know the war is over, certainly he does also. He will be on a boat out of Wilmington harbor before you boys reach Cross Creek."

Michael spoke softly. "But Mother, what shall we do?"

"You will each go into the bedroom and speak to Father. Perhaps it will comfort him that all of his children are here." Elizabeth paused. "And then there is a sad chore you must do. Our lumber was lost when the barn burned, but Mrs. Fritz says that they have plenty. The three of you must fetch enough to build a coffin for your father. And make it big and strong. He is a large man."

"No, Mother," cried Peter, horrified. Val and Michael were also upset, suddenly realizing the enormity of what had happened.

"Do as I say," said Mother. "It will be easier now than later. Now, go speak to your father."

Chapter 27

Grief

Her sisters were breathing quietly beside her in the bed they shared. Despite the grief of the day that had left the rest of the family exhausted, Eliza could not sleep. She was confused about exactly where Heaven was, and where Father would sleep and what he would eat there.

As she lay quietly, thinking about the things the minister had said at Father's funeral, she heard a noise. She had never heard it before, but it repeated again and again. It was coming from the other side of the main room. She climbed out of bed and tiptoed toward the sound.

The noise was coming from Mother and Father's room. As she neared the door, she realized to her amazement that it was Mother, quietly sobbing. She stood in the doorway, uncertain what to do.

Her mother sensed her presence and turned. "Little one, I am sorry you heard me. Now go back to your bed. It has been a hard day."

Eliza stayed in the doorway. "Why are you so sad, Mother? Father is with Jesus in Heaven, and happy there."

"So he is, child, and one day we will all see him again. But I cared for Father on this earth, and miss him sorely." Elizabeth raised herself on an elbow to speak.

"Mother, would you feel better if I slept with you?" asked Eliza.

"Perhaps so, little one, but you have your own bed. Give me a kiss and return to it. I must accustom myself to sleeping in this one alone." Elizabeth reached out her arms to hug Eliza, then sent her back to her room.

Chapter 28

The Will

"He is coming, Mother," said Peter. "I hear his horse on the path."

Elizabeth moved toward the door to greet their guest. Mr. Fritz dismounted and came onto the porch, a roll of parchment under his arm. "I hope the day finds you well, Mistress Leonhardt," he said solemnly, offering his hand.

"We are surviving, through the grace of God," replied Elizabeth, holding Mr. Fritz's hand in both of hers. They were old friends, but this was a day for formalities. "Please come in and take a seat." She ushered him to Valentine's chair before the fireplace.

Mr. Fritz began immediately with the business of the day. "Mistress Leonhardt, children, what I have here is a copy of Mr. Leonardt's last will and testament. He took the original with us to Salisbury when we went to join the militia and registered it with the county court there. We all did, and gave each other a copy. Peter, as soon as you are able, you must go to the court in Salisbury and swear to your father's death. Then the will will be recorded, and all of its provisions will become law. Now let us begin."

After locating his spectacles, Mr. Fritz removed the ribbon from the parchment roll and began to straighten out the paper. Elizabeth watched from her chair next to Valentine's, where Mr. Fritz now sat. Peter, Michael and

Val leaned against the wall, shifting restlessly. Barbara and Catherine sat on stools near their mother's feet, while the three smallest children sat wide-eyed on the floor. They were uncertain what was happening but knew it was important.

Mr. Fritz began. "I, Valentine Leonardt, being of sound mind and body, in this year of our Lord seventeen hundred eighty-one, hopeful of living a long life but headed into battle, do declare this to be my Last Will and Testament. My soul I commend to God, with the expectation that my family and I will someday again be joined in His Kingdom. Of my earthly possessions, I leave to my beloved Wife Elizabeth my manor house, all of my land adjoining Leonhardt Creek, and all of my personal property of any nature, for the remainder of her natural life, and upon her death, the title to the house and lands shall pass to my sons Jacob and Philip."

Peter flinched, but did not say a word. He had helped Father build this house and always assumed someday it would be his, not his little brothers. Were he and his older brothers to have nothing?

Mr. Fritz continued. "To my beloved daughters Barbara and Catherine, I leave to each the sum of fifty pounds in gold, to be paid from the savings I have accumulated as God has allowed me to prosper."

Both girls gasped. It was a fortune. Barbara could build her house with Thomas, and Catherine and Reid could move to Salem to start their inn and store.

Now, the three older brothers looked at each other with surprise. Father had always lived frugally, with no indication that he had significant wealth. But why did it all go to their sisters, and none to them?

Elizabeth was also confused. Why would Valentine have left nothing to their three oldest sons, who had worked side by side with him since they were small lads? And she knew of no gold.

"I suppose that is all, is it not, Mr. Fritz? That is more than we have ever had," sighed Elizabeth.

"Not quite, Elizabeth. There is next a provision that none of you may expect. Let me continue." Mr. Fritz found his place on the paper and read on. "I leave the five hundred acres of land that I have purchased, lying between Leonardt Creek and Abbotts Creek, to my sons Peter, Michael and Valentine, to be divided among such of them as shall survive me in equal shares, and direct that any remaining payment for the land be made from my estate before any other debt is paid."

The whole family was open-mouthed. The tract of land that Mr. Fritz was describing was the most prosperous in the county, with fertile soil and two deep creeks. It was enough land for the brothers to farm comfortably for the rest of their lives.

Elizabeth looked down at her youngest daughter, the only one not mentioned in the will. She was disappointed, but it was not serious. Valentine knew that she would always care for Eliza. She started to stand up.

"Wait," said Mr. Fritz. "There is one more line, added at the last." It says, "And to my beloved small angel, my cherub Eliza, I leave the sum of fifty pounds of gold, at such time as her mother determines it appropriate for her to have it."

The family was quiet for a moment, trying to comprehend all that they had just heard. Then Mother abruptly stood up. "That is all very nice, Frederick, but it is a fairy tale. We are ruined. All of our buildings save the house have been destroyed, the cattle driven off, and the entire harvest lost. We will live through the winter only on the charity of neighbors, God willing. My husband did not live long enough to make his dreams happen."

Peter spoke up. "Mr. Fritz, what do you know of this

land? When did Father buy it, and how much is still owed?"

Jacob could contain himself no longer. "Peter, Peter, there is something I must show you."

Peter turned, irritated. "Hush, boy, these are serious matters we are discussing here."

Mr. Fritz began to answer. "Your father bought this land several years ago with an agreement to make a payment each fall. The gristmill was more profitable than any of you ever knew, and your father was a shrewd horse and cattle trader. The last payment is due this December and the land would have been his."

Now Jacob was pulling on Peter's arm, trying to force him to come with him. "Peter, please come. Please."

Peter roughly pushed him to the floor. "Enough, Jacob, and do not say another word, or I will thrash you."

Jacob ran out the door onto the porch, sobbing uncontrollably. Father had told him what he must do, but he was failing at it. Inside, the discussion continued. "How much is this last payment?" asked Val.

"I am not certain, but I believe it is one hundred pounds. Your father planned to surprise all of you with this good news when the purchase was completed."

"Poppycock," said Mother. "Colonel Fanning took the few gold coins I had. If your father had more, I know nothing of it."

Jacob's sobs from the porch were audible inside the house, and Michael could stand it no longer. He stepped outside to console his little brother.

"Why are you so unhappy, little man?" asked Michael.

Jacob could hardly speak between sobs. "Michael, I know a secret, a very important secret, that Father told me before the war."

"I know, Jacob. Father was a great one for secrets. Once he showed me the cave where the bears go for the winter, and told me that only he and I would ever know this." Michael smiled at how Father had been able to make each of his children his special friend.

"Not that kind of secret, Michael, but a real one. He said that this secret is the future of our family. And Peter won't let me tell it." Jacob's sobs grew louder.

"Tell me, Jacob. You know I have always taken care of you." Michael pulled his little brother onto his knee, and rubbed his hair.

"I can't, Michael. That's not what Father said I must do." Jacob continued to sniffle.

"Then don't tell me the secret, but explain to me why you can only tell Peter," said Michael, suddenly more serious.

Jacob quieted, happy that someone was listening. "Father told me I could tell no one this secret until the fighting was over. And it is, isn't it, Michael? That's what the man on the road said."

"The fighting is over, Jacob. The British have surrendered, and we are a free state."

"That's one thing Father said, Michael. And the other is that when the war is over, Father said there is something I must show my oldest brother who came home. And that is Peter, and he won't let me show him." Jacob began to sob again.

"I understand, little man. Let's go back in the house."

They went back into the main room where the family was quietly talking, trying to figure out a way to make the last payment on the land so it would not be lost.

Michael spoke up loudly. "Peter, go with Jacob. He has something to show you."

Peter frowned. "Michael, quit letting Jacob pull your leg just because he is your favorite. It is time he learned to act like a boy while men are talking."

This time Elizabeth intervened. She looked at Jacob. "Is

this important, son?"

Jacob quietly nodded. Elizabeth smiled.

"Peter, go with Jacob and see what he has to show you," said Mother.

Peter protested. "Mother, I do not have time for children's games. We have serious issues to discuss here."

Elizabeth looked at Peter stonily. "While you were away soldiering, it was Jacob who rode through the night to fetch help for Eliza when she had the fever. And while you were hunting, it was Jacob who saved our horses when the barns were set afire. He is a brave young boy. Now do as I say."

Peter looked at Jacob coolly. "So what is this important secret, boy?"

Jacob took Peter by the arm and pulled him toward the stairs to the basement kitchen. "Come with me down the steps."

As they stood on the hearth, Jacob recited to Peter exactly what Valentine had said to him the year before. "Peter, count nine logs down from the top. Does that log look any different?"

Peter looked at the log quickly. "Of course not. I should know. I helped set it in place."

Jacob rushed on, eager to finally be rid of the secret he had carried for so long. "Now grab the tongs from the fireplace, place them on either side of the log, and pull."

Peter half-heartedly did as he was told, but nothing happened. "This is nonsense, Jacob. This is just some child's game that Father played with you."

"It is not. You're not trying, Peter. Pull hard, I mean, hard."

Irritated, Peter gave the log a hard yank with the tongs. To his amazement, a short piece dislodged from the wall and fell to the floor.

"What is this?" said Peter, confused. "I don't recall

using any short logs to finish the house. Father would never have let us do anything so shoddy."

Jacob picked up the log and smiled. "This is the secret, Peter. Feel how it is uncommonly heavy."

Peter took the log from Jacob, twisting it in his hands. "It is, little brother, but why?"

Jacob grinned as he pointed to the plug in one end. "Take that out and you will see."

Unable to remove it with his fingers, Peter grabbed one of Elizabeth's knives and gouged out the plug. He shook the log, and gold coins, hundreds of them, fell to the floor.

The brothers stared in amazement. Jacob started for the stairs, joyful to finally be free of the secret that had troubled him for so long. Peter called him back and put his hands on his shoulders.

"Jacob, I was wrong to be so cross with you. Father was right to trust you, and you have done well. Now run and tell Mother and the others to come here quickly."

Chapter 29

Moving On

"Before you leave, Peter, there is one more thing I must tell you." Elizabeth came out into the yard where Peter was mounting his horse. Now that the gold had been found, he was eager to get to Salisbury to record the will.

"Yes, Mother?" Since the episode with Jacob the day before, Peter had returned to his role as the responsible oldest brother.

"While you are in Salisbury, call on the Lutheran minister. Tell him we would be honored by his presence as soon as possible to perform the sacrament of marriage for your sisters. It is time."

Barbara overheard her mother and protested. "It is too soon, Mother. Catherine and I cannot leave you now, so soon after the loss of Father."

"Poppycock," said Elizabeth. It had become her favorite word. "When I was your age, I left my mother behind in Germany to travel here, and never saw her again. Your house will be scarcely a stone's throw down the creek, and Catherine less than a day's ride away in Salem."

Catherine joined the conversation. "Mother, I am not sure. Leaving all of you here seems too much." Tears ran down her cheek as she spoke.

"Nonsense, daughter. You are not meant for the life I

have lived. Go with Reid and live your own. If I could cross an ocean, you can go fifteen miles." Elizabeth placed her arm around Catherine's shoulders as she spoke. She saw in her second daughter the same spirit of adventure she had at that age.

Barbara was not persuaded. "But Mother, how will you manage on this farm, all alone?"

Elizabeth smiled. "I am not alone, dear. You and your older brothers will be close by, and I will live here happily with your little brothers and your sister. They grow every day, just as you did. And when they are old enough to make their own way, I will live out my days in this house your father and I built. He is in every log, and the creek is my comfort."

"Now go, Peter, you have important errands to do. And come inside, girls. It is time to spread breakfast." Elizabeth turned, and as she had on so many other mornings, headed into the house to feed her family.

Afterword

Valentine and Elizabeth Leonhardt emigrated from Germany, and raised eight children in their home beside what is now Leonard's Creek in Davidson County, North Carolina. Valentine and his three oldest sons fought with General Greene at Guilford Courthouse, and he was assassinated by Tories at the end of the war in retaliation for his role in persuading the German immigrant community to side with the rebels. Colonel David Fanning was a ruthless Tory leader who terrorized the Carolina countryside during the Revolution. There is no evidence that he was Valentine's actual assassin, but it is plausible.

Valentine is buried at Pilgrim Lutheran Church (first known as Leonhardt's Church) outside of Lexington, North Carolina. The dedication of an obelisk to his memory on the one hundredth anniversary of his death was attended by over 10,000 people. Although there are some early accounts that the famous "log safe" resides in the North Carolina Museum of History, the Museum can find no record confirming this.

The author, Rich Leonard, is a federal judge in Raleigh, North Carolina, who grew up in Davidson County. Valentine and Elizabeth Leonhardt were his great-great-great-great-great-grandparents.